Perhaps Love

Teena Raffa

ISBN: 978-0-9953976-9-9

Perhaps Love

$\mathscr{L}$OVE. Now there was a four-letter word that was well and truly over-used. I shook my head as I scanned the text on my computer screen. The romantics of the world had a lot to answer for. *Love forever. Love everlasting. Love eternal.* Really? As if. I gave what my mum would have described as an unladylike snort, then leaned in to correct a typo.

Just as well my opinion on the existence of true love didn't creep into my writing or my career as a romance novelist would be over. I re-read the last few lines I'd written.

'Happy?' The look in Ben's eyes made Tessa's heart sing.

'Blissfully,' she said as he reverently touched the gold band on her finger before wrapping her hand in his.

She settled back in her seat, a-glow with the wonder of it. Ben loved her. They were man and wife. Tomorrow they'd touch down in Paris, the most romantic city in the world.

Who would have thought love would tap her on the shoulder in the frozen foods section of the local supermarket? She'd believed romance was dead. How wrong she'd been. It was very much alive. And Ben had promised to prove it to her every day for the rest of their lives.

A new day was dawning as the plane lifted into the sky and carried them into tomorrow.

Sweet. That'd do it. I typed 'The End', saved *Winter's Dream* to my DropBox and a USB stick and closed the document. Another Melanie Ames 'romantic read for loving hearts'. The satisfaction of a job well done lasted all of six seconds. An image of a silhouetted couple locked in a passionate embrace at the ocean's edge at sunset now filled my screen. I sagged down in my chair with a sigh. It was all so easy in fiction. If only there were happy ever afters in everyday life. Why couldn't I conjure up a Mr Wonderful for myself like I did for the characters in my novels?

Maybe if I believed in the fairy tale it might happen for me. But I didn't. Sean the Lying Cheating Bastard saw to that. Four years with him killed any idea I'd ever had that true love and real romance were anything but a beautiful fantasy. It was bad enough he conned me out of my savings. Finding out he had another fiancé on the other side of the country plus regularly indulged in one-night stands with any babe who caught his fancy opened my eyes to the truth.

Thanks to him I'd become a cynic of the first order. It was difficult to pretend excitement when friends and relatives shared their engagement news and wedding plans. When the invitations turned up I hesitated to accept. I wasn't sure I could trust myself not to leap up and interrupt proceedings to beg the besotted couple to come to their senses.

How could they vow to love each other forever? It simply wasn't possible. Maybe for generations past. Not now. The evidence was everywhere. They only had to look around. Marriages don't last. Relationships only survive for as long as it takes one partner to decide someone else can make them happier. The bliss is fleeting. The magic is a myth.

I shrugged away the thoughts. Enough of the negativity. This had to stop. Okay, my characters had happy ever after and I didn't. That's life. Best get over it. What I needed was physical activity to get myself moving and clear my head. I'd spent too many hours at the computer. No wonder my body had seized up and my brain was throwing up negative thoughts. A bike ride should do the trick.

I headed for the bedroom to change out of my PJs. Shakespeare meowed in protest as I shifted him from his cosy nest on my clean clothes in the rocking chair by the window. He leapt onto the unmade bed to circle and claw the bunched up quilt before settling once more.

'You've got it made, cat,' I said as I wriggled into a pair of tights and pulled on a T-shirt. 'Sleep and eat, eat and sleep. What a life.'

I ducked down to fetch my sneakers from beneath the bed. By the time I bobbed up again, his eyes were closed.

'Great company you are.' I sat on the edge of the bed to put on my socks. 'Lift your game, boy, or I'll trade you in on a more companionable companion.'

My threat was wasted. He didn't stir, so I got on with the job of lacing up my sneakers.

On my way out of the room, I said, 'I'm going for a bike ride. Won't be long.' Then I rolled my eyes at the ceiling. I was telling my cat that? There was no question about it. I had a serious case of cabin fever. A change of scene was well overdue.

I wheeled my bike out of the shed and onto the patio. It was a sorry sight after years of neglect. The purple frame was dulled by a layer of dust, spider webs festooned the spokes and both tyres were completely flat. I hadn't ridden it since I was a teenager. Why I'd thought to go for a bike ride today instead of a brisk walk was a mystery. Perhaps being back in Mum and Dad's house had flicked my nostalgia switch. I'd always loved riding my bike along the beach path, coasting down the hills, swooping round the bends, setting myself the challenge of making it up the hills without dismounting to push up the last of the slopes.

I went indoors to fetch a brush, a cleaning cloth and Mum's sewing machine oil and set to work. Fortunately my old pump was still attached to the bike frame but I'd forgotten what hard work it was. By the time I finished making the bike roadworthy I was beginning to think that was quite enough physical exercise for one day.

Then a tiny wagtail hopped onto the nearest grevillea and cocked its head at me as if to say, 'What? Giving in so soon?' How could I resist a challenge like that?

I locked the back door, hid the keys under one of Mum's pot plants, buckled on my helmet and wheeled my bike out through the side gate and onto the drive.

There was a removalist van at the house next door. I vaguely remembered hearing a truck earlier but I'd been too deeply involved in Ben and Tessa's story to look through the front window and check what was going on. I laughed softly. Definitely not my father's daughter in that respect. He kept a close eye on goings on in the street, could tell you who'd bought a new car, been away, had unfamiliar visitors, mowed their lawn. He'd definitely have noticed new neighbours were moving in to the vacant house next door. That's one of the downsides of being a writer with a head full of stories. Life can pass you by if you don't watch out.

Today I was doing something about that. This would be fun. I knew I'd heard somewhere that once you learned how to ride a bike you never forgot how to do it. Maybe, if I was lucky, that wouldn't be all I remembered. My poor scarred heart might even remember how to love again.

Sure! And the tooth fairy wasn't a fantasy. Pigs could fly to the moon. My head certainly needed clearing. The sooner this bike ride was under way, the better. Swinging up onto the bike, I settled into the saddle and glanced to the right to check the road was clear. There should have been a 'Danger Ahead' sign. 'Man at Work' would have helped.

The mere sight of the removalist was a major health hazard. Dressed only in butt-hugging jeans slung low on lean hips, his tanned chest and arms rippled with muscles as he effortlessly hoisted a small timber chest from the back of the truck onto his shoulders.

My bike wheels wobbled. Struggling to maintain control, I swerved to miss the letterbox. Diving headlong into Mum's bush garden was not on my agenda for today. I gripped the steering wheel and resisted the urge to shut my eyes and pray. Though I might have squealed, 'Oh my god.' And maybe He heard, for suddenly I was back on track. Disaster avoided. With a whooshing breath of relief I careered into the street and set my sights on the road ahead.

But not before I caught a quick glimpse of an amused grin and received a cheeky salute from Mister Muscle. Huh? I snorted and shook my head. He thought he'd caused my near collision with the letterbox? Not a chance. As if a good-looking guy with the body of a Greek god would put me off balance. I'd learnt from experience. Bad boys came in good packages.

I was simply out of practice. It had been at least a decade since I'd ridden a push bike. And what a glorious day for it. Blue skies. Sunshine. Okay. It was winter. There wasn't much warmth in that sun. But there was nothing like a bit of exercise to raise a body's temperature and the crisp

August air felt welcomingly cool on my flushed face as I pedalled along the Fendam Street footpath.

It was relatively quiet on this weekday morning. There was almost no traffic and few people were about. I moved off the path onto the road for a dog walker and later an elderly man shuffling along in his slippers, saying a cheery 'Good morning' as I passed.

I'd no sooner congratulated myself for doing such a wonderful thing for my body and mind than my legs began protesting at the unfamiliar demands. By the time I'd passed the roundabout and started pedalling up the hill to the bike path along Warnbro Beach Road my under-exercised lungs had me gasping for breath. I'd forgotten how much effort it took to ride a bike without any gears. Surely it wasn't good for my heart to be bumping about in my chest this way.

I braked, dismounted and pushed the bike the rest of the way up the hill, puffing all the way. It was such a relief to reach the top and collapse on the conveniently placed seat. Dragging off my helmet and fanning my face with one hand while I caught my breath, I pledged to do something about my fitness. Judging from this morning's effort, my nanna was probably in better physical shape than I was. I'd make bike riding a regular part of my daily routine, maybe book into a gym. If I wanted to live long enough to write all the stories running through my head I needed to take better care of myself.

The water in the bay shimmered in the sunlight. Gulls wheeled and swooped and a couple of pelicans soared majestically by, but I failed to spot any dolphins despite squinting out to sea for what seemed like ages. Taking a deep breath of the sea air, I closed my eyes and enjoyed the sun's warmth on my face for a few minutes more. Then I replaced my helmet and set out on the return journey. All I could think about as I rounded the corner into our street was how lovely it would be to collapse on my bed and recover.

My heart sank when I saw the removal van was still outside the house next door. I hoped Mister Muscle was inside shifting furniture about. Even though seeing him had had nothing whatsoever to do with my almost disaster earlier, I knew I'd blush if I saw him again because that's what *he* thought. My plan was to get indoors as quickly as possible without risking an encounter.

But as I dismounted and started to wheel the bike up the drive, I saw he and his offsider were sitting in the back of the van taking a drink break. Mister Muscle grinned and waved. Heat rushed to my face. That meant I was beet red. I cursed my Celtic ancestors for the lily white skin I'd inherited, wished myself invisible and looked straight ahead after responding with a quick nod. With a bit of luck, he'd not noticed my blush. Now all I had to do was open the gate and get round the back and out of sight.

It didn't take me long to realise there was a problem with that. I'd shut the gate with the lever that lifted the latch to open it on the inside rather than the outside. At 'five foot and an onion', as my departed great grannie would have said, I wasn't tall enough to reach over the top of the gate to lift the latch. How was I supposed to get round the back to get the keys and let myself inside? The gate on the other side of the house was padlocked on the inside. It too was a couple of metres high and built of Colorbond. Darn Dad and his obsession with security.

There was only one thing for it: to get back into the house I had to climb the fence. That wouldn't have fazed me if I'd been one of those people who spent their childhood being adventurous. I read books. I didn't climb trees, use the clothes hoist as a tightrope or scramble onto the roof of the garden shed to check the weather. I left that to my brother. But how hard could it be? All I had to do was leap up, get a grip on the top of the fence with both hands and swing first one leg, then the other, up and over. Easy peasy. I hoped.

Stepping back, I took a deep breath to prepare myself, then leapt at the fence.

'Need a hand there?' asked Mister Muscle, who'd strolled over to see what I was doing.

'Or two?' sniggered his offsider, joining him at the low side fence that separated Mum and Dad's property from the neighbour's.

What? They thought I was a pathetically helpless female who couldn't scale a fence without some guy's help? My characters climbed mountains. I didn't. But I could surely manage a six-foot Colorbond fence.

'No thank you,' I said.

'You sure about that?' asked Mister Muscle as I struggled to hoist myself off the ground.

'Perfectly,' I said with as much dignity as I could muster now that I'd managed to get one leg over the fence and the other trapped by the foot in the branches of the hibiscus that grew at the side of the house. I gave my foot a good hard tug. That freed it right enough. But a jagged branch, left no doubt by Dad's pruning saw, refused to give in without a fight. It snagged my leggings and held fast. My face felt like it was on fire. Bad enough that I was stuck with one leg on either side of the fence. Why did I have to have an audience? I tugged … and tugged again.

'You sure you don't want a hand there?' His voice was as disarmingly attractive as his body. Under other circumstances I'd have wondered if that wonderful lilt was Irish. Now I had another priority.

'I—can—manage,' I huffed out, and with one final tug my tights came free with a loud ripping sound and I toppled over the fence and landed on the brick paving round the back with a thud and a loud, 'Umph.'

His face appeared above the fence. 'You all right?'

I stopped groaning and rubbing my left rump. 'Yes.'

'Sure and I'm pleased to hear it,' he said.

And then he was gone.

I buried my head in my hands and sat there feeling sorry for myself. Exercise was supposed to be good for you, not leave you in worse shape than before you started. Not only had I earned myself a whopping great bruise on my backside, I'd ruined my favourite floral leggings.

The phone ringing indoors put a stop to the inspection of my injuries. It was the landline, so I knew it wouldn't be my publisher or one of my friends but nonetheless it got me moving. Of course, by the time I'd retrieved the key from its hiding place in the pot of azaleas, unlocked the back door and limped to the hall table, the caller had hung up without leaving a message. Thank goodness for call logs. It was Nan doing her grandmotherly duty and checking in to make sure I was okay so I called her right back.

'Hi, Blossom,' she said, 'I thought you must be busy writing.'

I lowered myself carefully to the floor and settled in for a chat. 'No. I finished the book I was working on and I'm taking a break before I get on with the next one. I went for a bike ride.'

'Did you?'

I know I usually exercised my brain and my fingers more than the rest of my body, but she needn't sound quite so surprised.

'It's a gorgeous day and I thought I ought to get some exercise.'

'An excellent idea. I'm sure it can't be good for you to spend so much time at the computer. You could always come to my boot scooting class. It's a lot of fun.'

The thought of my seventy-something grandmother jigging about in her jeans and cowboy boots to Country and Western music with a group of other senior citizens made me smile.

'I'm sure it is, but I think I'll stick to bike riding for now. And you don't need to worry. I'm doing fine.' I decided not to mention my less than happy encounter with the side fence. 'The house is still standing and Mum's pot plants seem to be surviving her absence without ill effect.'

'Have you heard from them lately?'

'Unfortunately, Nan, the pot plants and I aren't on speaking terms.'

'Don't get smart, Bloss, you know what I mean.'

'Sorry. Not since Dad sent those photos of Uzbekistan. They're probably out of range and don't have access to WiFi.' I could almost hear the worry wheels turning and thought I'd best put Nan's mind to rest. 'Really, Nan, I'm sure they're fine. It's a guided tour. They're not going to take them anywhere dangerous. I'm sure Mum and Dad are having an awesome time.'

'Yes, well, I do hope you're right. Anyway, that wasn't why I rang. I've just made a delicious tofu and vegetable curry and I thought you might like to come round for lunch.'

'That would be lovely, Nan. Give me half an hour or so to have a shower and change, and I'll be there.'

It would cover two bases. One: Nan could rest assured she was fulfilling her promise to Mum that I wouldn't waste away from lack of a decent, home-cooked meal while they gadded about the planet on their six-month trip of a lifetime; and two: Mister Muscle and his moving van mate should be long gone by the time I returned and there'd be no risk of further embarrassing encounters.

I spent the afternoon at the computer helping Nanna to create a photo book for her boot scooting class's fifth anniversary so the sun had lost its warmth and it was almost six when I returned home. The house next door could still have been vacant from outward appearances. The newcomers must have tucked themselves in for an early night after the exhaustion of moving day, though I did notice a light on in the house as I waited in the kitchen for the kettle to boil for my Cup-a-Soup. I wondered briefly about what sort of people they were but really, it wasn't relevant. I was only house-sitting for Mum and Dad so was unlikely to have much to do with their neighbours.

I was rather tired myself so meandered through the evening, answering emails, reading a few blogs about writing and cruising Face Book before changing into my PJs and tucking into bed with a novel. No sooner did I switch off the lamp and snuggle under the covers than the barking started. Not an occasional yelp or a minor woof. This was a full volume, big dog brand of bark and it was nonstop.

At first I tried to ignore it, concentrating on my breathing, bringing my attention into the room, trying to block out the sound. It didn't work. Neither did getting up and stomping over to shut the bedroom door or burying my head under both the pillow and doona. My sympathy for the poor creature getting used to unfamiliar territory quickly dissipated and gave way to a rising anger at its inconsiderate owners. What was wrong with them? They must be able to hear it. Did they really think allowing their dog to wake the neighbourhood was the right way to establish a friendly relationship?

Hours of wakeful tossing and turning fed my temper and in the early hours of the morning I dragged myself to the computer, switched it on and printed out the council's dog laws and some information about Bark Busters. While it was still dark I marched out the front and stuffed the pages into next door's letterbox.

Second thoughts had set in by the time I'd drunk my first coffee of the day and I wished I'd not been so hasty. But it was now daylight and there was no way I was going to risk being seen raiding their letterbox to retrieve what I'd posted in it. I popped a slice of bread in the toaster and hoped the person who'd made the early morning mail delivery would remain a mystery to them. The dog had finally stopped barking, so I also hoped last night was a one-off occurrence while it settled in to its new home.

With a bit of luck it had worn itself out as well as me and I'd have the peace and quiet I needed to start the next book. Considering I had the freshness of a leaf of wilted lettuce after my sleepless night, writing the opening chapter of a new story was the last thing I felt like doing. I reminded myself I was a professional author with a four-book contract and headed back to the computer. A quick check of my emails showed the copy edits for Book Two in the Seasons of Dreams series had arrived. I smiled and opened the file. It was earlier than expected but a task much better suited to my current fragile state of mind. Lack of sleep doesn't agree with me. I knew I'd have the creativity of a gnat. The new novel could wait.

Perhaps Love

My peaceful morning lasted till about eight thirty. I heard next door's garage door open, a car pull out of the drive and the door close behind it. The departure was followed almost immediately by loud yelps of protest. The yelps became barks. I groaned and buried my head in my hands. How was I supposed to work with this incessant noise? The poor creature wanted company and everyone in the neighbourhood was going to hear about it.

Perhaps it would settle down if I popped my head over the fence and spoke to it. I stomped through the house, out the back door and into the yard. Being a shortie, I couldn't see over the fence while standing on the ground so I started to cart across one of the plastic chairs from the patio, thinking to use that for added height.

Suddenly the barking increased in tempo, there was the sound of thundering feet and something big and heavy thudded against the other side of the fence. A huge beastly head appeared above the fence line. It had a mouthful of teeth in a gigantic jaw. That was all the warning I needed to keep my distance. I screamed, dropped the chair and abandoned all thought of befriending the creature. Given half the chance it would probably eat me for breakfast. At Olympic gold medal speed I was back inside and leaning against the sliding glass door panting.

The dog was now barking louder and thundering up and down the yard on its side of the fence. How was I supposed to think, let alone work? There was only one thing for it. Taking a deep breath and reminding myself I was a brave and courageous woman and not a timid wimp,

I made a lightning dash for the shed. Dad wore earmuffs to protect his hearing when mowing the lawn. They could serve my purpose just as effectively.

In record time I was back at the computer, working happily on my copy edits and feeling rather pleased with myself for having solved the noise problem. I'd also decided that unneighbourly or not, I'd give the newcomers a week. If their nuisance dog hadn't settled down by then I'd call in the big guns. The council ranger could sort it.

I became so engrossed in what I was doing that fresh air and exercise didn't enter my mind. Neither did lunch or what was happening in the world away from my computer screen. Eventually, though, I became conscious of the tightness in my neck and shoulders. Hunger pangs reminded me I'd eaten nothing but a slice of toast and vegemite and half a dozen almonds since about six am. It was now almost dinner time. Such a star effort deserved some reward. Pizza? Fish and chips? Chinese or finger lickin' chicken? Decisions, decisions. I saved my work and shut down the computer. A yawn and a toe-touching stretch later and I was ready to go check the letter box and water Mum's pot plants on the front porch.

Within minutes I was regretting setting foot out the front door. The beast from next door was on the loose. Our eyes met and it headed straight for me. I didn't wait to find out if it planned a welcome or an attack. With an almighty yell, I took a running jump for the top of the brick letterbox. Fear gave me skills I hadn't known I possessed and I actually made it, but what safety I thought it would afford me, I have no idea. I was beyond thinking rationally and motivated by sheer terror.

'Cat! Sit!' called a commanding voice. To my amazement the monster instantly skidded to a halt and sat back on its haunches, though it kept me under surveillance, tongue out and drool dripping from its open jaws.

I stayed put. I'm not a risk taker. Propping both hands on my hips, I turned my attention to its owner. 'What the hell do you think you're doing letting this—this beast loose in the street? It could have killed me.'

'She's harmless. She wouldn't hurt a flea.' The Irish lilt did nothing to calm my rage.

'Famous last words,' I snapped.

'The worst she'd do is lick you to death.' He ambled up to the animal, knelt down and fondled its head to prove his point. 'Wouldn't you, you big wussy girl?'

In reply, the big wussy girl slurped his face with that enormous tongue.

It didn't convince me. 'Yeah. Right,' I said. 'Just be warned. If this happens again, I'll be on the phone to the ranger. There are laws about dogs in suburbia.'

'Ah.' He nodded. 'So it was you.'

The guilty flush no doubt gave me away. Nonetheless I maintained my dignity.

'Take it away now, please,' I said.

'Sure.' He shrugged, rose to his feet and clicked his tongue. 'C'mon, Cat. Home, girl.' The dog obediently padded after him.

I waited till they'd reached the front door and watched him open it and let the dog inside before deciding it was safe to climb down off the letterbox.

As I bent over to check for mail I felt his eyes on me and glanced across to the house next door. He was leaning against the verandah post, grinning.

'Cute outfit,' he said.

That's when I realised I was still wearing my PJs.

It took me much longer to realise a much more significant detail than what I was wearing.

The evening had turned chill and Shakespeare and I were tucked under a rug in Dad's recliner chair in the lounge watching a repeat episode of Midsomer Murders when my brain belatedly clicked into gear. Mister Muscle was not the removal guy. He was the new neighbour. I almost choked on a mouthful of rice cracker and hummus so made a quick grab for my glass of lemonade on the floor near the chair. This dislodged Shakespeare from his comfy spot on my lap. He landed on the floor with a miaow of protest, gave me a reproachful look at such disrespectful treatment and stalked towards the doorway.

'Don't blame me, cat,' I called after him. 'It's him next door who's to blame.'

What a moron, I thought. Dangerously good looks obviously disguised a brain the size of a lentil. Even I could work out something as basic as giant-size dog plus dwarf-size side gate equals escape. The man didn't have a clue about being a responsible, community-minded pet owner. And who in their right mind would call a dog Cat? Thank goodness I only had to put up with him and that monster in the short term. If he could manage to keep it under control for the next six weeks, we'd get along just fine.

I scooped up a generous dollop of dip on a cracker and settled back to watch Inspector Barnaby solve the latest Midsomer murder. During the ad breaks I amused myself by devising interesting ways to finish off Mister Muscle if he and his dog disrupted my life any further.

The next few days were unexpectedly peaceful. My sleep was undisturbed thanks to Dad's ear muffs. Rain, wind and cold banished all thought of bike rides or brisk walks and I happily tucked myself away indoors and powered away at my writing commitments. Once the copy edits were done I got to work on the first draft of the next book.

My only outing was a trip to the shops to buy some more paper for my printer and restock my supply of rice crackers and dip. As I pulled out of the drive I noticed a king-size gate had replaced the original one next door. That earned Mister Muscle a mental tick of approval for doing one right thing. Pity he hadn't done anything to deal with the overnight barking and daytime whining. He had two days left to improve his game before I followed through and called the ranger. I had no plans to make ear muffs a permanent fashion accessory.

Mum called from their hotel in Kazakhstan. 'Everything all right?' she asked.

'Fine. My agent likes the new book, Nanna's been making sure I get at least one home-cooked meal every week, your azaleas are in full bloom and Dad's lawn is probably the greenest in the street after all the rain we've had. Oh, and by the way, next door is no longer vacant.'

'Lovely.' I could hear the smile in her voice. My mum the befriender. 'What are the neighbours like?'

Now that was a leading question. 'It's a guy and his dog,' I said. Why spoil her holiday with worries about nuisance neighbours? 'I've not had much to do with them.' It was true to a point — and if I had my way, that's how it would stay.

After Mum's call I abandoned my fantasy world for a reality break. The sun was shining and a crisp breeze had flicked my hair in my face when I went out the front to pick up the local paper from the driveway. The perfect day to do a load of washing. Mum's dryer had packed up long ago and not been replaced and I was almost out of clean knickers and leggings. A dose of Vitamin D probably wouldn't go amiss, either, so with thoughts of lunch and a book on the deck, I loaded the machine and did my version of housekeeping.

Shakespeare watched me make the bed, flick the furniture with a duster and give the bath a quick clean, then followed me to the kitchen and supervised sandwich making and tea brewing from his stool at the breakfast bar. Satisfied all was up to standard, he went to have a snooze on the cane sofa in the family room.

'Not going to make sure I unload the machine and hang out the washing properly?' I asked on my way to the laundry.

He opened one eye, then closed it again and curled into a tighter ball.

'I take it that's a no.'

Sad, I thought as I loaded the clean clothes into the laundry basket. I was so desperate for company I was expecting reasonable replies from a cat. Hoisting the basket onto my hip, I opened the sliding glass door and stepped outside.

A loud thud came from the direction of the back yard and I stopped and listened. What was that? Thinking the wind had toppled one of the pots on the deck, I placed the basket in the trolley and walked round the side of the house to check. The pots were all in place. I turned away and walked back to the clothes line fixed to the side of the house.

Thud! It came again. Thud, thud, thud, thump! I frowned, then shrugged. Mister Muscle must be doing something next door. I took a pair of tights from the basket and reached up to peg them onto the line. The thumps and thuds continued. Uh oh. Was that what it sounded like? Darn right! I froze. The beast from hell was taking running leaps at the fence. It was trying to get into our yard. There was no way I was going to wait and find out if its next attempt worked. The washing could wait. Safety first was a much better idea. I dashed towards the open laundry door.

Too late! The dog called Cat landed in our yard with a crash and came thundering round the side of the house. I gave an Oscar-winning shriek and cringed against the brick wall, fearful for my life. But she galloped right by me and hurtled through the open laundry door with a triumphant bark, claws skidding on the wet tiles. A terrified yowl from the family room sent a chill up my spine. Shakespeare! I had to save him.

I hurled myself through the door. My right foot missed the step. My left slipped in the puddle on the floor. A quick grab for the side of the sink prevented me from doing the splits. There was no time to stop and catch my breath. Shakespeare streaked along the passage towards the guest bedroom. The dog called Cat was in close pursuit, barking frantically.

'Sit!' I yelled. It had worked for Mister Muscle.

It didn't work for me.

I panted after her. Shakespeare had taken refuge on top of the wardrobe and was huddled way back against the wall. The beast had leapt onto the bed and looked like it was about to try its chances at the wardrobe next.

'Cat …' My voice came out in a frightened squeak. 'Here, girl … come on …'

I might as well have been talking to myself. She didn't take her eyes off the top of the wardrobe.

I could have grabbed her by the collar, hauled her off the bed and dragged her outside. I'm not brave. Neither am I stupid. I want to live with every limb intact. There had to be a less dangerous option.

Of course! Food. I backed along the passage one careful step at a time, then ran to the kitchen and pulled open the fridge door. Thank goodness I hadn't eaten all last night's takeaway chicken dinner. This should do the trick — I hoped.

Before I'd even shut the fridge door the dog called Cat had got a whiff of what was on offer. I barely had time to scrape the leftover vegies and a chunk of breast meat onto the floor before she bounded up and wolfed it down. Several tiles licked cleaner than they'd been since Mum and Dad left on their travel adventure, she sat back on her haunches and looked at me with her tongue hanging out and drool dripping out of those big scary jaws. I thought quickly. The only other thing I could give her was half a packet of rice crackers. It would probably buy me maybe five minutes to figure out how to get her out of the house.

I caught a sudden flash of white fur escaping through the still open laundry door. Shakespeare had obviously decided outside was safer than inside.

Unfortunately the beast was on the ball. Or more precisely, on the trail. Food forgotten, she gave chase, with me close on her tail. I didn't know if Shakespeare had enough of a head start, couldn't bear the thought of him being caught and ripped to pieces. I skidded round the side of the house in time to see him leap from the side fence to the top of the shed. Relief surged through me. He was safe.

Dad's vegie garden at the side of the fence, however, was at risk of total destruction. Frustrated her prey was beyond capture, the dog called Cat was leaping around like a maniac, trampling everything underfoot.

'Sit!' I yelled. 'Stop! Come!' Even if she'd heard me above her frantic barking I doubt anything I said would have stopped the rampage.

I collapsed into one of the cane chairs on the deck and burst into tears. What else was a girl to do?

'Stop! Enough!' The stern command from the other side of the fence shocked me and the dog to silence. I hiccupped on a sob. She whined and flopped down in the trampled mess of dirt and plants. Mister Muscle hoisted himself up to scale the fence and land in our yard among the grevilleas. I'd never been so glad to see anyone in my life. My first impulse was to fling my arms around his neck and smother that criminally good-looking face with kisses for coming to the rescue. Under the circumstances that wouldn't do.

I sprang out of my chair and stalked over to where he was now standing on the lawn surveying the damage his dog had caused. Said creature was quietly lying at his feet, looking for all the world as if she wasn't responsible for any of it.

Hands on hips, I glared at him. 'Your dog is a menace and you don't deserve to be a pet owner.'

'I'm so sorry,' he said.

'Sorry? Sorry! Is that all you can say?' I could hear my voice rising to a shrill crescendo but could do nothing to stop it. My hands too seemed to have a will of their own and were gesticulating wildly. 'She's completely wrecked the vegie patch. Look what she's done! Ruined it. And poor Shakespeare. He's so traumatised he's probably going to have a heart attack and die.'

Mister Muscle looked a bit confused. 'Um—he is dead. Long dead.'

I shook my head. 'Not that Shakespeare. My cat. He's up there.' I pointed to the top of the shed.

The summer sky eyes with the fringe of dark lashes cleared in understanding and he nodded. 'Ah.' He stared up at the shed roof. Shakespeare was a tight-curled ball of white fur right in the centre. 'I see.'

Unfortunately so could I. All he was wearing was a pair of denim shorts. They hugged that neat butt and rode low on those lean hips I'd found such a safety hazard days earlier. His shirtless torso sported the most impressive six-pack I'd ever seen this close and my misbehaving heart immediately started a soft shoe shuffle. This would not do. I forced myself to lift my gaze above his neck but the slightly crooked smile and twinkle of amusement in those startlingly blue eyes set my face on fire.

I cleared my throat. 'Well. Sorry is just not good enough. I've been more than patient about the night and day barking and your dog getting out and scaring me shitless the other day. This—' I waved both arms around to take in the trail of damage. '—it's—the last straw. Clearly you can't control your dog. I'm going right inside to call the ranger.'

The smile disappeared. So did the amused twinkle. 'Please …' he said, reaching out and touching me on the arm, 'I know she's trouble but this dog means the world to me.'

I didn't know whether it was the lovely lilting accent or his touch that sent a tingle right down to my toes and melted my heart. Or it might have been the soulful look the dog called Cat was giving me as she lay so well behaved at his feet.

'Um—ah—' For a writer I was surprisingly lost for what to say next. We stared at each other wordlessly. I looked from him to the dog and back again. Which of them looked the most pleading was debatable.

'I'll fix things,' said Mister Muscle. 'I promise.'

'Good.' My ability to speak had returned. 'You can start with the yard. But I don't want that dog here while you do it.'

He ran a hand through his dark curls and gave me a disarming grin that turned my legs to jelly. 'Great. I'll take her home and put her inside, then come back and get your yard looking as good as new.'

I raised my eyebrows at him. Really? I didn't think so. Not unless he could turn back the clock an hour or so. There'd be precious little vegies from Dad's patch this season.

He shrugged and laughed, a deliciously throaty sound that made me think of decadent desserts. 'I'll do my best. Come, Cat.'

She obligingly rose to her feet and followed him towards the side gate.

I trotted after them. 'Um—Cat? You're not worried about giving your dog an identity crisis?'

He flashed me that heart-stopping smile and paused with one hand on the gate and the other resting affectionately on the dog's shaggy head.

'Her name's Catalpa. After the ship used in the Fenian escape. Would you know the story?'

I did. A small group of Irish prisoners had organised a daring escape from Fremantle Prison and sailed to freedom in a ship that waited off the coast of Rockingham. 'There was quite a bit about it in the local paper when the council had that memorial put up at Palm Beach.'

'The flying geese.'

'Yes. So—you'd be Irish then?'

'I would.'

It still seemed an odd thing to call a dog. Maybe Houdini would have suited her better. She was definitely an escape artist. Considering the creature in question was now investigating my crotch with interest, I decided to leave further interrogation of its owner for some other time. Perhaps. If Mister Muscle lived up to his promise of making amends and ensured there weren't any repeat performances of today's disruptive incident.

I backed away from the beast. 'Um—uh—well, just come back through the gate when you're ready. There are gardening tools in the shed. I'll leave it unlocked.'

He nodded and led the way next door, Catalpa padding obediently at his side. Anyone passing by would have thought she was the best behaved dog in the world. I knew better. I simply had to look at the state of our backyard. Shaking my head, I hitched the side gate open for Mister Muscle's return and went to unlock the shed. Shakespeare was still on the roof.

'You can come down,' I told him. 'You're safe now, she can't hurt you.'

He wasn't convinced. All I got was a plaintive meow. He didn't even uncurl. I sighed and went inside to see what damage repair needed to be done in there. With Mister Muscle due back any minute I didn't want to be caught midway through a cat rescue operation. Shakespeare had got himself up on the shed roof without any trouble. He'd come down when he was ready.

It didn't take me long to restore order in the house. The hat stand in the corner of the family room had been knocked over but fortunately it had fallen away from the wall so the plaster was unscathed. I set the stand back in place and gathered up the scattered hats, caps, scarves and brollies. The wardrobe in the guest bedroom, however, had a permanent reminder of Catalpa's uninvited visit. Shakespeare had left long scratches in the door as he slid to the ground to make his getaway while the dog was in the kitchen. Furniture polish helped a little but the scratches were there to stay. Thank goodness my mum had a forgiving nature. I'd have to figure out how to soften the blow for Dad over his vegie patch, though. With a sigh I stripped the dirty bedlinen from the bed and took it to the laundry to load the machine. While the wash cycle was under way I quickly gave the laundry, passage and kitchen floors a mop over, then slipped outside to resume hanging out the clothes I'd washed earlier.

I knew Mister Muscle had returned and was working in the yard but I'd refused to give in to the temptation of watching that amazing body in action through the back window. Now I resisted the urge to take the few steps along the side of the house and sneak a peek, concentrating instead on pegging each item carefully to the line. Finally, the last pair of knickers was flapping in the breeze. I mentally congratulated myself. A hot male bod merely metres away and me sex starved for months, yet I'd shown remarkable restraint.

A polite cough interrupted my thoughts. I peeled one wet leg of a pair of tights from around my neck and tried to look composed.

'All done?'

'All done.'

'Right then.' I emerged from among the laundry and followed him to inspect the results of his labour.

'Sorry about your vegie patch,' he said as we stood side by side at the edge of the neatly raked ground with its sparse scattering of surviving plants. A few hours earlier it had been a thriving bed of silver beet, tomatoes and broad beans and I'd been so proud of myself for keeping it that way in the weeks I'd been housesitting. My dismay must have shown on my face, for Mister Muscle had the grace to look contrite. He touched me lightly on the shoulder. It sent a jolt clear through me and I jerked away as if I'd had an electric shock. Luckily he thought it was because I was upset about the vegies and launched into further apologies.

I stopped him. 'Look, what's done is done. And I appreciate that you've made an effort to fix the damage.'

'It was the least I could do.'

'Right—well—'

All he had to do was smile at me and there I was, mumbling away again like an inarticulate moron. Did he have to stand so close? I was eye to tanned, muscular chest. 'Uh—thanks,' I managed at last. It came out as a squeak and I cringed.

He ran his fingers through his hair. 'I'll be off then.'

He strode towards the gate and I trotted along behind him. It was only polite.

Suddenly he stopped and turned and I narrowly avoided a collision.

'I'm Liam,' he said.

'Melanie,' I replied. 'Pleased to meet you.'

'But not my dog.'

His tone was serious but the amused twinkle in his eyes was a giveaway and I smiled.

'I'll reserve my opinion on that count.'

'Fair enough.'

He pulled the gate shut behind him and I was left standing there feeling unexpectedly lonely.

I headed for the shed to see if I could entice Shakespeare down from the roof. He wouldn't budge, even when I went inside and returned with treats. After a while I gave up. I also gave up any idea of writing more of my book. For some inexplicable reason my green-eyed blond Aussie corporate executive hero had acquired tousled dark curls, blue eyes and an Irish accent between one chapter and the next. The day was a write off. I couldn't get my brain back in gear. The memory of Mister Muscle's big mitt wrapped around my small paw kept sending rushes of delicious warmth through me. It was ridiculous. I must be completely starved of human contact.

With that in mind, I called my housemate Sofie to see if she wanted to take in a movie or go out for a drink but she had plans. We settled for a long phone chat. I didn't mention Mister Muscle.

After our call I tried unsuccessfully to coax Shakespeare down from the shed and then again at dinner time. No luck. As far as he was concerned, ground level was seriously dangerous. He was staying put. By this time it was dark and cold and I had no intention of staying out there all night sweet talking a cat.

Inside, though, I couldn't settle. I kept jumping off the sofa where I'd settled with a book, a sandwich and a cup of hot chocolate, thinking I'd heard his collar bell at the side door. It wasn't much better when I went to bed. Between fantasies about a devastatingly attractive Irishman sweeping me into his arms to claim my lips, and imagining I'd heard Shakespeare meowing to come in, sleep completely eluded me.

At first light I was back outside searching everywhere for my missing cat. At some stage during the night he must have ventured down off the shed roof but he wasn't answering my calls. I looked in all his usual hiding places without finding him. Where was he? Standing in the middle of the backyard, I gave in to anxiety and frustration and let the tears fall. After a bit I dashed them away with the back of one hand and glared at the house next door.

This was all *his* fault. And his dog's. So what if he had a heart-melting smile, a lilting voice that made a girl go weak at the knees and a body to swoon for? If he was a more responsible pet owner — if he'd kept his monster of a dog under control and not let it leap into my yard and go on a rampage through my home and property — I wouldn't be missing one beloved cat that had been irreparably traumatised by the experience.

I ignored the small point that it wasn't actually my home or property that had been rampaged through; and that said cat wasn't technically mine either any longer, since it had continued to live here with Mum and Dad after I moved out five years ago to house share with Sofie, who was terribly allergic to cats.

A plaintive cry from the roof of the patio interrupted this trail of thought and relief rushed through me. I'd found him! He was safe! I hurried over to the edge of the patio and looked up at him with what must have been a Cheshire cat size grin.

'There you are!' I said, stating the obvious. 'There's a good boy, come on down.'

He meowed a rather long reply. Fortunately I had a good understanding of cat language and realised immediately he was telling me he was an indoor cat, unused to the outdoors. While he'd got up there easily enough, he wasn't sure he could get down.

That fazed me. Along with not being brave, I don't do heights. There was no point me fetching the ladder from the shed. I'd be having a dizzy spell before I'd reached the top rung. As for climbing onto the roof to rescue Shakespeare, that was likely to lead to a disaster of the first order. There was only one thing to do. Mister Muscle had caused this dilemma. He could solve it.

I did have enough presence of mind to change out of my pussy cat print PJs before marching next door and pressing his front door bell. I'd clearly woken him up because he looked deliciously sleep tousled when he peered round the partly opened door.

'What's up?'

'My cat. He's on the roof of the house and I need you to get him down.'

He frowned in confusion. 'Me?'

'Yes, you. I don't do heights. Anyway—' I tossed my head. 'It's your fault he's up there. It's your fault he's been out all night without any dinner. If your dog—'

'Okay. You've made your point. Give me five minutes to get some clothes on.'

Oops. He really had just crawled out of bed to answer the door. My face burning with embarrassment, I backed away, almost missing my footing and landing in among the daisies. I pointed in the direction of my place. 'Um. I'll go get the ladder out of the shed.'

'Good idea,' he said and shut the door.

Ten minutes later I was holding the ladder steady for him — he'd said there was no need but I didn't want any accidents — and trying not to let my mind wander into dangerous territory. Even though that hot bod was now adequately clothed in a T-shirt and jeans, the rear view was disconcerting to say the least.

'He's moved up further onto the main roof,' said Liam, interrupting my thoughts and prompting a quick side step to avoid butting his backside with my nose as he backed down the ladder.

'We need to shift the ladder round the side of the house so I can climb up and get him.'

'Right.'

'Is he likely to scratch me to pieces when I try to grab him?'

Good question. 'Um—I don't think so. He's usually really gentle.'

'Let's hope he lives up to that reputation.'

Liam smiled and my heart skittered. The weeds in the brick paving suddenly required my urgent attention. I bent down to pull them out while he set the ladder against the side wall and climbed onto the roof. I couldn't watch him up there anyway. I'm as queasy watching people scale great heights as I am about being high off the ground myself so I kept my back turned till I heard him return safely to the ground, murmuring softly to Shakespeare.

'There you go,' he said, handing him over. 'Safe and sound, and neither of us the worse for wear.'

I snuggled Shakespeare close. 'Thank you. We're very grateful. Aren't we, boy?'

Liam leaned against the wall. He looked in no hurry to leave. I looked down at the cat purring contentedly in my arms. It felt like the safer option. I didn't like the way my body was responding to the proximity of the man next door.

'I hope we haven't made you late for work.' It seemed like a polite way to hurry his departure.

But he made no move to go and merely gave another of those now-familiar smiles, which had the usual result of turning my insides to marshmallow.

'I work from home. No one to answer to, and I'm in no rush.'

The Irish lilt didn't help matters. My mouth felt like the Sahara and I swallowed. Thank goodness my hands were firmly fastened around Shakespeare or who knows what they might have decided to reach out and touch.

'And you?' One dark eyebrow lifted questioningly.

'I work from home too. I'm a writer.'

'How about that. Me too. What do you write?'

I lifted my chin, instantly in defence mode. 'Romance.'

'Whoa!' He held up one hand and grinned. 'Back off, Rocky. You won't get any crap from me. I know how much work goes into writing a book. I'm a journo but I'm also a wannabe novelist. I've just hit the 25,000 word mark of a historical novel and it's been bloody hard getting my butt into gear to get this far.'

And a bloody nice butt it was too, I couldn't help thinking, though I kept my sights firmly fixed above the neckline of his body-hugging tee. Common sense warned me to stop. Hit the brakes. Change gear. Reverse.

My errant heart refused to listen and I found myself asking Liam if he'd like a cup of coffee.

I knew I was in deep trouble when he said, 'I've got a better idea. Why don't we go to one of the cafés at the foreshore, have breakfast and get to know each other? If we're going to be neighbours …'

'Actually, we aren't. Not for long, anyway. This is my parents' place. They're on holiday in Europe at the moment and I'm looking after it while they're away.'

He shook his head. 'Curiouser and curiouser.' At my surprised look, he added, 'Yes, I have read Alice in Wonderland. My mum's absolutely passionate about literature and she introduced my sisters and me to all the classics. So we have more in common than both being writers and owning troublesome pets—'

'Shakespeare's not troublesome.' At the sound of his name, the cat in question decided to leave the safety of my arms and amble casually over to the patio door to sit waiting expectantly for me to let him indoors. I was otherwise occupied, pretending interest in brushing white fur from my black top.

'Feisty little thing, aren't you?' said Liam.

'Not usually. Just setting the record straight.' I gave up trying to restore my top to its pre-Shakespeare cuddling appearance and drew circles in the dust with the toe of my ballet flats instead. 'You were saying?'

'I'm only here temporarily, too. My aunt's bought the place. She's still finalising things at her old place so she's not ready to move in for another few weeks. She knew I was doing a lot of research into the Fenian escape for my novel and suggested I stay here in the meantime. It suits us both – Auntie Maureen gets to have the house occupied and I get a bit of a feel for this place where it all happened. What do you say, then?'

'About what?' I was so lost in the summer sky depths of his eyes and the music of his voice I'd completely lost the plot.

'Breakfast.' Those vivid blue eyes were alight with mischief. 'If you've an appetite.'

Oh I had an appetite all right. And it was embarrassingly R-rated. Breakfast sounded like a wonderful appetiser.

'I'll put Shakespeare inside and make myself presentable.' I must look a mess after dragging the ladder out of the shed and assisting with cat rescue.

'You might want to do that.' He leaned forward and flicked something from my cheek with one finger. His touch was electric. I shivered. His voice dropped to a husky murmur. 'And I've been wanting to do this from the moment I first saw you wobbling towards the front letterbox on your bike.'

He placed one hand gently beneath my chin, tilted me face up and lowered his lips to mine. I made no protest, simply surrendered to the sweet promise of that kiss.

'Ten minutes?' he said and stepped back.

Tipsy with the intoxication of his touch, I took a moment or two to catch my breath and recover my balance. 'Make it fifteen.' I smiled up at him. 'Your car or mine?'

'Yours, if that's all right. Mine's not in a fit state for passengers at the moment, what with the move and all and Cat not being such a good traveller.'

'Where do you live?' There was so little I knew, so much I wanted to know.

'Serpentine. I've five acres. I like space around me and it's good for Cat too. Plenty of room for her to roam. She's not liking being in a small backyard and I wouldn't do it to her except it's only in the short term. Putting her in a kennel or having her stay with friends wasn't an option. She frets when she's away from me.'

Sweet. The bond between a man and his dog. 'She's been quiet so far this morning.'

Liam grinned. 'She's in the laundry with a king-size bone. For sure, it'll keep her happy while we're out. You decide where you'd like to eat and I'll be back directly.'

This time when I fastened the gate after he'd left, it wasn't loneliness I felt but a thrill of excitement. Hurrying indoors, I fed a ravenously hungry Shakespeare, had a lightning-fast shower and changed into a pair of jeans and a sweater that I knew flattered my curves. All thought of word counts, rewrites and publisher deadlines was completely abandoned. Real life was more important than fiction. I was going to have breakfast with a gorgeous hunk of a man who apparently was also intelligent and interesting, and who knew where that would lead?

Maybe I'd been too quick to decide true love was a myth. It might be possible after all. My dormant heart had woken with a jolt, kissed to life by an Irishman with a voice like warm honey and a dog called Cat. My romance novelist's brain skipped ahead to misty, rose-coloured scenarios of Liam and me walking hand in hand along the sandy shore of the bay as dawn broke over the ocean and the rising sun tinged the sky with a peach glow. It conveniently ignored the reality that the path ahead might be rocky from time to time. For now, it was blissfully happy living in the moment. It was way too early to tell if Liam and I had a future together. But it turned out I wasn't such a cynic after all. I was open to possibilities and more than ready to believe love could be more than a myth.

Teena Raffa

Thank you for reading *Perhaps Love*

We hope you enjoyed it.

If you enjoyed it, please consider leaving an honest review on

Goodreads or Amazon. Reviews can help readers find books and

we would be grateful for your help. Thank you for taking the

time to let others know what you thought.

If you'd like to know more about Louisa, or connect with her

online, please visit her webpage teenaraffamulligan.com, follow

her on Twitter @traffam, or like her Facebook page

https:// www.facebook.com/TeenaRaffaMulligan/

This book was published by Serenity Press under its Serenity

Romance imprint. If you'd like to see what else Serenity Press

publishes, visit serenitypress.org

Teena Raffa

Teena Raffa is a reader, writer and daydream believer who believes there is magic in every day if you choose to find it. She discovered the wonderful world of storytelling as a child and decided to become a writer at an early age. Teena writes for children and adults and her publications range from poetry and short stories to picture books and a middle grade novel. Her writing life has also included a long career in journalism. She shares her passion for books and writing by presenting talks and workshops to encourage people of all ages to write their own stories. Her website is www.teenaraffamulligan.com

www.ingramcontent.com/pod-product-compliance
Lightning Source LLC
Chambersburg PA
CBHW020624120726
47905CB00003B/930